How does it look?

Bobbie Kalman
🌳 Crabtree Publishing Company
www.crabtreebooks.com

Created by Bobbie Kalman

For Kathy Kantor, an amazing designer,
and an even more amazing human being! Thank you for being you.

**Author and
Editor-in-Chief**
Bobbie Kalman

Editors
Reagan Miller
Robin Johnson

Photo research
Crystal Sikkens

Design
Bobbie Kalman
Katherine Kantor
Samantha Crabtree (cover)

Production coordinator
Katherine Kantor

Illustrations
Barbara Bedell: page 24 (ladybug)
Anne Giffard: page 7 (snakes)
Katherine Kantor: pages 5 (shapes), 6, 7 (lines), 17 (spirals),
    24 (lines and circle)
Bonna Rouse: page 18

Photographs
© BigStockPhoto.com: page 9 (top)
© iStockphoto.com: page 13 (left frog)
© 2008 Jupiterimages Corporation: page 22 (boy)
© ShutterStock.com: front cover, pages 1, 3, 4, 5, 7, 8, 9 (bottom), 10,
    11, 12 (all except bottom right), 13 (all except left frog), 14, 15,
    16 (background), 17 (all except water), 18, 19, 20, 21 (all except
    right frog), 22 (all except boy), 23 (animals), 24 (all except frog)
Other images by Comstock, Corbis, Creatas, and Photodisc

Library and Archives Canada Cataloguing in Publication

Kalman, Bobbie, 1947-
    How does it look? / Bobbie Kalman.

(Looking at nature)
Includes index.
ISBN 978-0-7787-3315-7 (bound).--ISBN 978-0-7787-3335-5 (pbk.)

    1. Pattern perception--Juvenile literature. 2. Color in nature--
Juvenile literature. 3. Nature--Juvenile literature. I. Title.
II. Series: Looking at nature (St. Catharines, Ont.)

BF294.K34 2007   j508   C2007-904236-8

Library of Congress Cataloging-in-Publication Data

Kalman, Bobbie.
    How does it look? / Bobbie Kalman.
        p. cm. -- (Looking at nature)
    Includes index.
    ISBN-13: 978-0-7787-3315-7 (rlb)
    ISBN-10: 0-7787-3315-7 (rlb)
    ISBN-13: 978-0-7787-3335-5 (pb)
    ISBN-10: 0-7787-3335-1 (pb)
    1. Pattern perception. I. Title. II. Series.

BF294.K35 2007
152.14'23--dc22

                                    2007026953

Crabtree Publishing Company

www.crabtreebooks.com   1-800-387-7650
Copyright © **2008 CRABTREE PUBLISHING COMPANY**. All rights reserved. No part of this publication may be reproduced, stored in a
retrieval system or be transmitted in any form or by any means, electronic, mechanical, photocopying, recording, or otherwise, without the prior
written permission of Crabtree Publishing Company. In Canada: We acknowledge the financial support of the Government of Canada through the
Book Publishing Industry Development Program (BPIDP) for our publishing activities.

**Published in Canada
Crabtree Publishing**
616 Welland Ave.
St. Catharines, Ontario
L2M 5V6

**Published in the United States
Crabtree Publishing**
PMB16A
350 Fifth Ave., Suite 3308
New York, NY 10118

**Published in the United Kingdom
Crabtree Publishing**
White Cross Mills
High Town, Lancaster
LA1 4XS

**Published in Australia
Crabtree Publishing**
386 Mt. Alexander Rd.
Ascot Vale (Melbourne)
VIC 3032

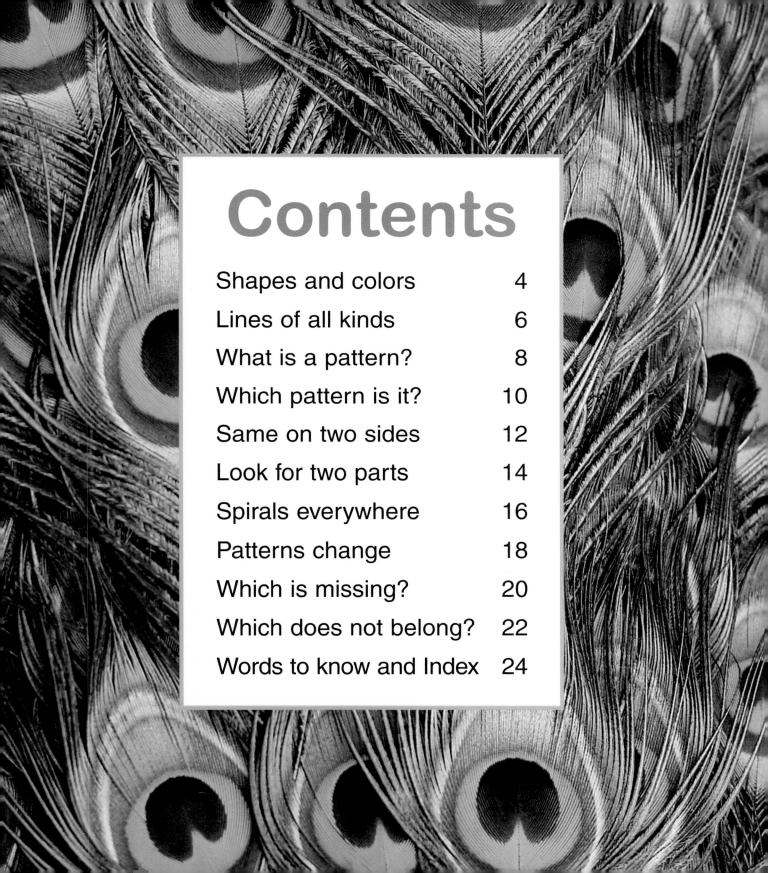

Contents

Shapes and colors

Everything has a color. Everything has a shape. What shape is the Earth? Name three colors you see in this picture of Earth.

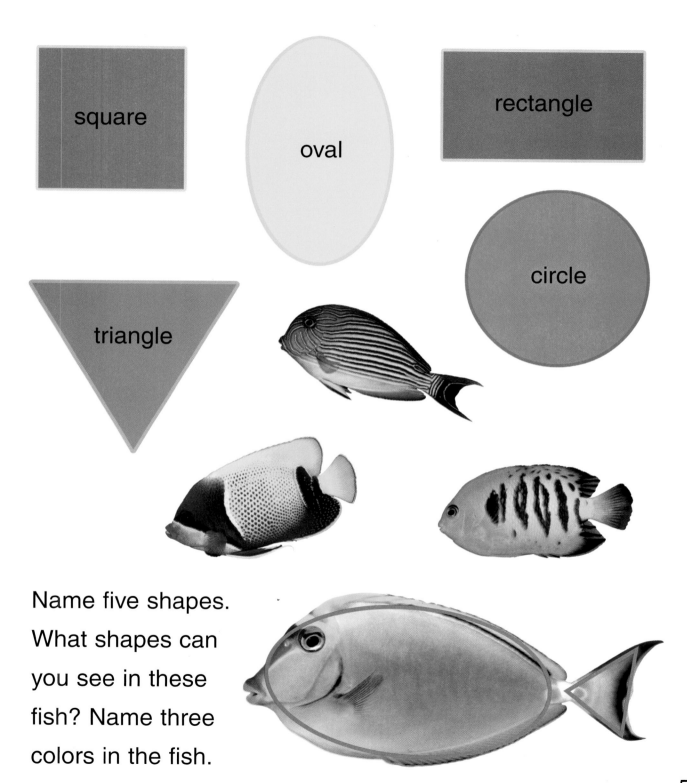

square

oval

rectangle

circle

triangle

Name five shapes. What shapes can you see in these fish? Name three colors in the fish.

5

Lines of all kinds

Shapes are made with lines. Squares, rectangles, and triangles have **straight** lines. Circles and ovals have **curved** lines. Lines can be thick or thin.

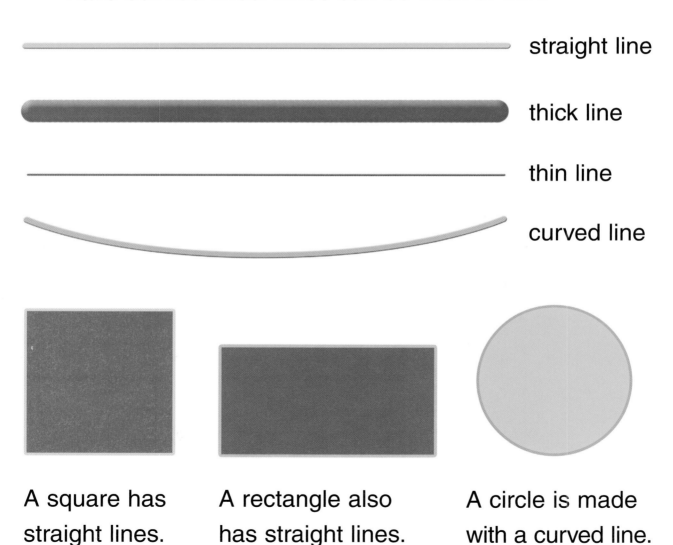

straight line

thick line

thin line

curved line

A square has straight lines.

A rectangle also has straight lines.

A circle is made with a curved line.

There are also **spiral** lines, **wavy** lines, and **zigzag** lines.

spiral line

wavy line

zigzag line

Which animals are moving in wavy lines?

Which animal has a spiral line on its body?

Which animal has a zigzag line on its body?

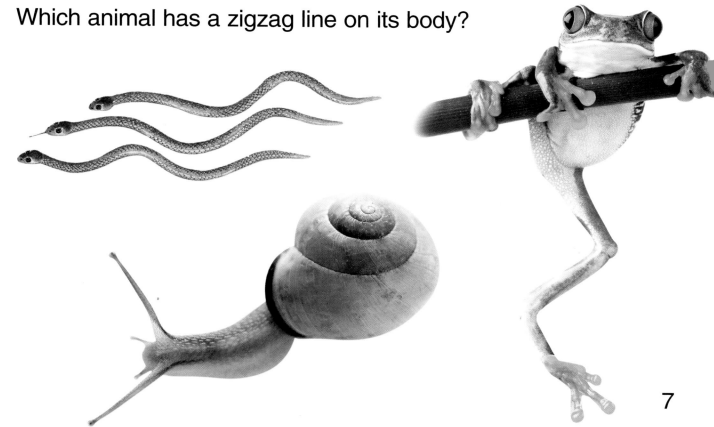

7

What is a pattern?

Everything has a **pattern**. A pattern can be made up of lines, shapes, and colors. The lines, shapes, and colors in a pattern repeat. Many animals have patterns on their bodies.

This zebra has many black **stripes** on its body. Some of its stripes are thick lines. Some are thin lines. The zebra's stripes make a pattern on the zebra's body.

This frog has a
pattern on its body,
too. What colors are
in the pattern? How is
the frog's pattern like
the zebra's pattern?
How is it different?

Name five colors on this fish. What makes
up the pattern on its tail? Did you say
spots? What shape are the spots?

Which pattern is it?

Look at the patterns below. Match them to the animals on the next page. Which two animals have stripes? Which animal has spots? Which two animals have the same colors?

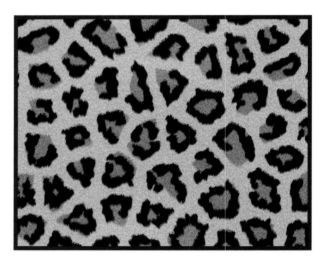

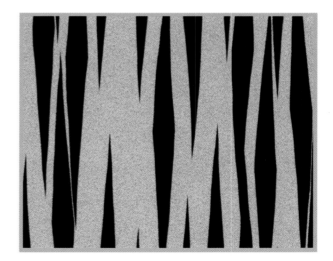

10

giraffe

tiger

leopard

zebra

11

Same on two sides

Some animals have the same parts or patterns on both sides of their bodies. Butterflies have two wings. When a butterfly folds its wings together, it looks like it has just one wing. The butterfly's body has **symmetry**. Symmetry is having the same parts on both sides.

The patterns on the butterfly's wings are the same on both sides.

The bodies of many
animals have symmetry.
Frogs have symmetry.
Birds have symmetry, too.

Look for two parts

People have two sides, too. Both sides of our faces are almost the same. What is in the center of your face? Which parts of your face are on each side of the line?

Our bodies have symmetry, too. We have two arms and two legs. How many fingers do you have on each hand? How many toes do you have on each foot?

Spirals everywhere

Spiral lines start at a center and get bigger
and bigger. Spiral shapes are everywhere!

Hurricanes and tornadoes have spiral
shapes. This picture shows a hurricane.

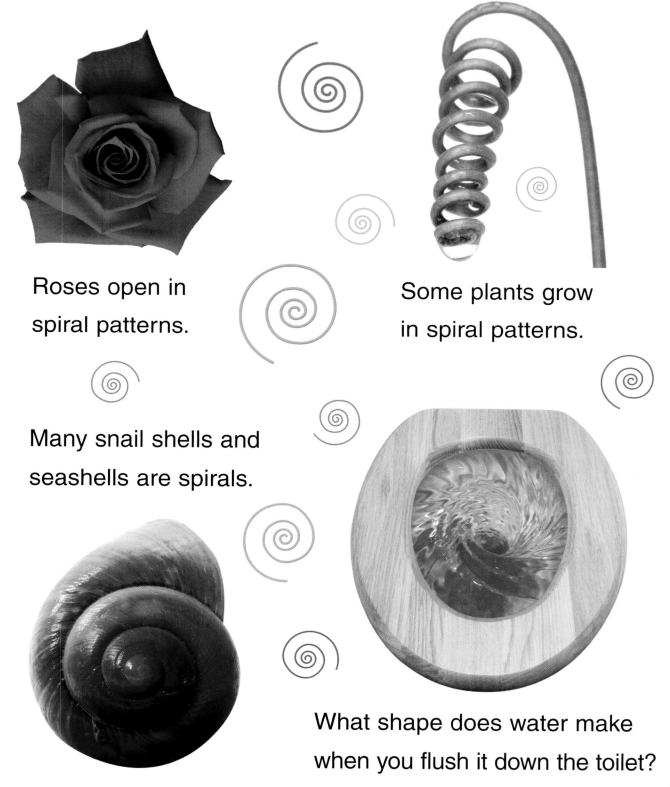

Roses open in
spiral patterns.

Some plants grow
in spiral patterns.

Many snail shells and
seashells are spirals.

What shape does water make
when you flush it down the toilet?

17

Patterns change

This flower is pink. It has a
yellow center and a green stem.
There is a bee on the flower.

18

There are many pink flowers above. Each flower has a bee on it. The flowers and bees make a pattern. Is the pattern the same in the picture below? How has the pattern changed?

Which is missing?

Each group of these animals forms a **set**. One animal is missing from each set. Find the missing animals on page 21.

set 1

These animals are **reptiles**. Which animal belongs here?

set 2

These animals are **birds**. Which animal belongs here?

20

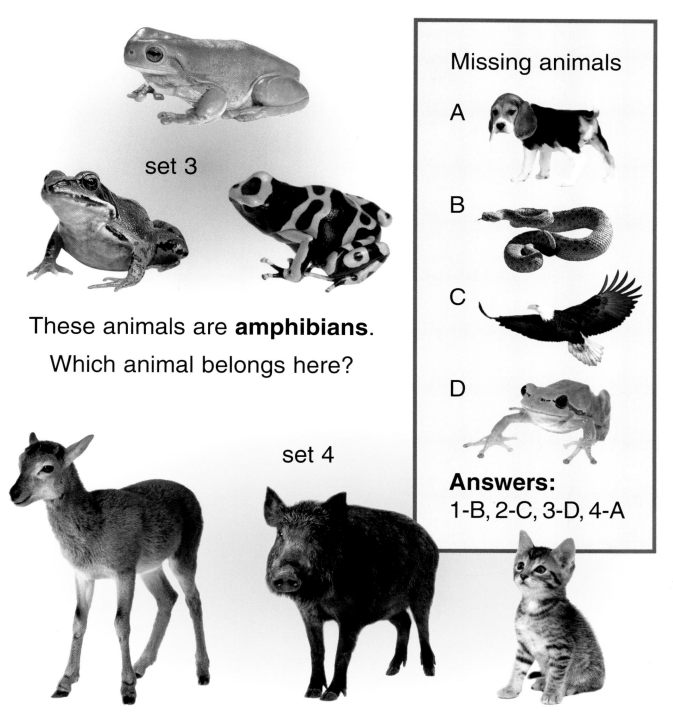

set 3

These animals are **amphibians**.

Which animal belongs here?

Missing animals

A

B

C

D

Answers:
1-B, 2-C, 3-D, 4-A

set 4

These animals are **mammals**. Which animal belongs here?

Which does not belong?

Which of these things does not belong in the first set? For a clue, see pages 16-17.

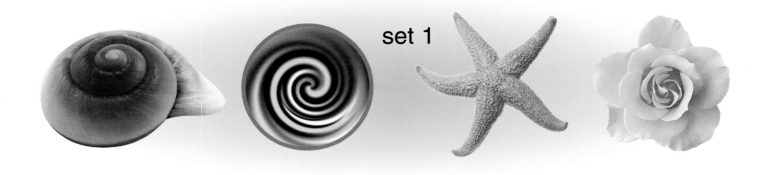

set 1

Which does not belong in the second set? For a clue, see pages 12-15.

set 2

Which fruit does not belong in this set?

For a clue, see pages 4-5.

set 3

Which pattern does not belong?

For a clue, see pages 8-9.

set 4

Answers:
1. The sea star does not have a spiral shape.
2. The flower does not have symmetry.
3. The banana is not round.
4. The ladybird beetle has spots, not stripes.

Words to know and Index

colors
pages 4-5, 8, 9, 10

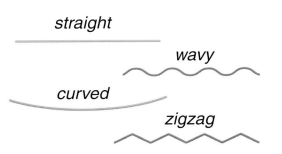

straight

wavy

curved

zigzag

lines
pages 6-7, 8, 16

patterns
pages 8-11, 12, 17, 18, 19, 23

sets
pages 20-23

circle

shapes
pages 4-5, 6, 8, 9, 16, 17, 23

spirals
pages 7, 16-17, 23

spots
pages 9, 10, 23

Other index words

stripes
pages 8, 10, 23

symmetry
pages 12, 13, 15, 23

Printed in the U.S.A.